NATURE

✳ A MAGICAL ✳ JOURNEY THROUGH THE YEAR

Sara Conway

Illustrated by
Lee Foster-Wilson

◼SCHOLASTIC

Published in the UK by Scholastic, 2021
Euston House, 24 Eversholt Street, London, NW1 1DB
Scholastic Ireland, 89E Lagan Road, Dublin Industrial Estate,
Glasnevin, Dublin, D11 HP5F

Text written by Sara Conway
Illustrations by Lee Foster-Wilson
Helen Bostock – RHS Senior Horticultural Advisor
Andrew Salisbury – RHS Principal Scientist Entomology

ISBN 978 0702 30237 4

A CIP catalogue record for this book is available from the British Library.

Printed and bound in China by C&C
Paper made from wood grown in sustainable forests and other controlled sources.

2 4 6 8 10 9 7 5 3 1

www.scholastic.co.uk

RHS

Inspiring everyone to grow

NATURE

✳ A MAGICAL ✳ JOURNEY THROUGH THE YEAR

CONTENTS

THE JOURNEY BEGINS

This book is a journey through nature in its many forms. A journey can mean time spent moving between two places. You might make a journey on two feet or on two wheels, visit a local park or a faraway land. But often you can take a journey in a spiritual sense, too, when a change inside you alters the way you see the world. We hope this book will take you on both types of journey.

These pages will lead you to different natural places. You'll experience the world season by season, climate by climate; visit a garden waking from winter, paddle at the beach, dance with autumn leaves and stop to rest by a frozen pond. You'll meet creatures living in steaming rainforests, and ones that thrive in dry deserts. And you'll see the world differently too, travelling beneath the soil and above the clouds, burrowing with earthworms, soaring with birds and looking closely at everything: from the smallest seed to the tallest tree.

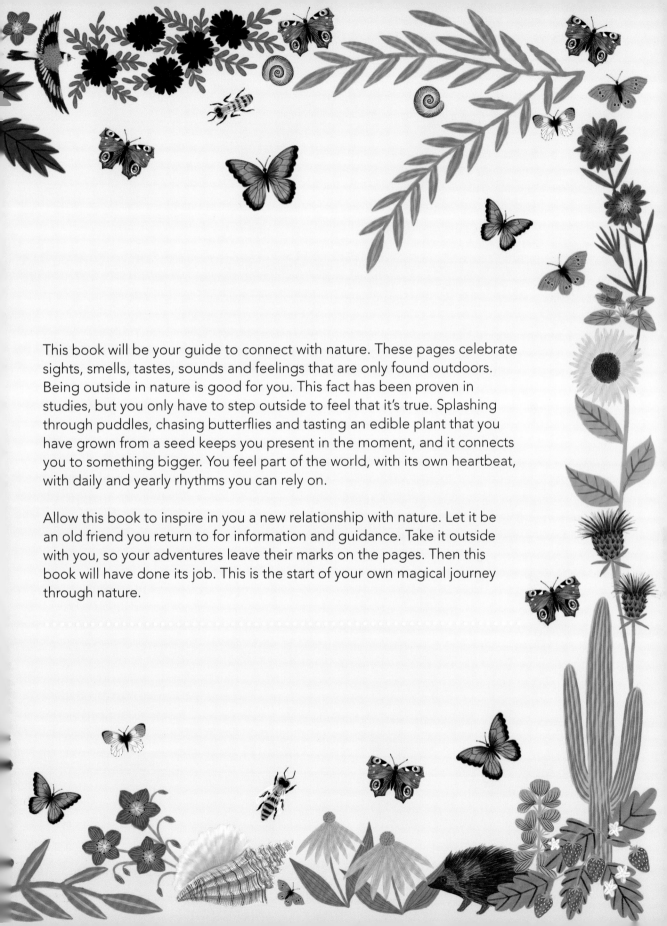

This book will be your guide to connect with nature. These pages celebrate sights, smells, tastes, sounds and feelings that are only found outdoors. Being outside in nature is good for you. This fact has been proven in studies, but you only have to step outside to feel that it's true. Splashing through puddles, chasing butterflies and tasting an edible plant that you have grown from a seed keeps you present in the moment, and it connects you to something bigger. You feel part of the world, with its own heartbeat, with daily and yearly rhythms you can rely on.

Allow this book to inspire in you a new relationship with nature. Let it be an old friend you return to for information and guidance. Take it outside with you, so your adventures leave their marks on the pages. Then this book will have done its job. This is the start of your own magical journey through nature.

SPRING

SPRING

A season for new beginnings, springtime is the perfect time for plants to begin growing again as the weather becomes warmer. For weeks, the Sun will shyly show its face, only to be followed by more wind and rain. Then, one day, spring will nudge its way in at last. The Sun will warm your back and you'll take off your winter coat, happy to have your arms swinging freely once again. And, just as you peel off your layers, plants unfurl in the sunshine, too: leaves open, buds burst out and bare trees start to turn green.

Spring is when the world comes alive. Some animals wake up after a long winter sleep; there is a sense of purpose and activity as homes are built and new lives are created. Soon, young animals will be leaping in the fields and hidden seeds will sprout, becoming a flower, something to eat or the start of a great new tree.

In this section, you'll walk through gardens, woods and wetlands, stopping to feel the changes taking place. What are your favourite parts of this season? Perhaps you know them already. If not, you're bound to discover them waiting for you outside. Now, is the time to feel the stickiness of chestnut buds on your fingers, see colourful springtime bulbs warming the end-of-winter days, and spot the first brave insects emerging into the warmer sunshine. Perhaps you'll beat them to it.

THE FIRST SIGNS OF SPRING

Springtime starts with a snuffle, a hedgehog's nose close to the ground. A drip of melting ice that plops next to shuffling paws. Indoors, they don't hear quiet changes: drip, drop, rustle, gurgle. You, with your mud-caked wellies, ears to the air. You hear it first. Spring is here.

Like a spell lifting, a garden seems to come to life all at once. Snowdrops are one of the first flowers to appear in spring. These small, white bell-shaped flowers may look dainty but don't be fooled – not many flowers can bloom in the cold.

Waking from a winter sleep, a root pushes down and a shoot unfurls, looking for sunshine. These shoots will soon grow into bright, sunny daffodils. Spring will transform the trailing branches of the silvery catkins from silver to yellow as the pollen is released.

Animals and insects wake after their long winter sleep. A queen bumblebee will soon take flight and find the perfect place to nest. A hedgehog has finished hibernating and is looking for breakfast – a tasty earthworm will do.

NEWBORN ANIMALS

Is there anything sweeter than the lamb with her wagging tail or the owlet with her big wide eyes? Is there anyone busier than the sheep or the owl, hunting, feeding, carrying, cuddling? Funny to think these parents were the newborns once, in a not-so-long-ago spring.

Lambs feed from their mothers. As the spring days get warmer and longer, female sheep spend their days eating lots of fresh grass so they can make milk for their lambs. The youngsters butt their head against mum until the milk flows.

Owls are talented hunters, but nest builders they are not. Owls often use rot holes in trees and can use woodpeckers' abandoned nests. Woodpeckers peck holes in tree trunks to nest and lay their eggs, moving on when their chicks become fledglings and are able to fly.

LISTEN: MIGRATION

They're here! Filling the air with their song. Brave travellers, they've crossed desert and sea, followed moon and stars, to land in your back garden. Fling your arms wide and sing to them, I hear you! You're here!

Birds sing mostly at dawn. Male birds usually sing the loudest to mark their territories against rival males. As there are so few other sounds that early in the day and the air is so still, the birds' song carries a lot further than it would later in the day.

As the days get shorter and colder, a bird's senses tells it when it's time to migrate. Before migration, many birds start to fly restlessly; they form flocks and they feed, feed, feed before the long journey.

Birds use landmarks, such as forests, mountains, and the Moon and stars, to help them find their way. Some birds can use the Earth's magnetic poles to navigate over areas that don't have many landmarks, such as the ocean.

Some birds fly between countries in spring to find food, a safe place to nest and raise their chicks. They do it all over again in autumn to find a warm home and food for winter. A willow warbler only grows up to 13 centimetres (5 in), but it flies 5,000 miles (8,000 km) from Africa to the UK during migration.

Cuckoo

Chiffchaff

Swift

Swallow

House martin

Osprey

Nightjar

Flycatcher

Yellow Wagtail

BIRDS' NESTS

Swiftlet

The birds are busy building. No bricks, mortar or hard hats – nature's recyclers, they pluck rubies from the rubble. A twig, blade of grass, a slick of saliva, feather, lick of mud, thread from a spider to build a home, cosy and strong, ready for their eggs.

A swiftlet's nest is made with materials, such as feathers, paper, hay and anything else the birds can carry. The materials are glued together by drops of their parents' saliva, which hardens to create a shell.

Ruby-throated hummingbirds create little cup-shaped nests to cradle their chicks.

Mistle thrushes often use human rubbish, including plastic and waste paper, to build their nests.

Baya weaver birds craft a teardrop-shaped nest by weaving together grasses with their beaks.

Bald eagles need a great, big nest. They carry large twigs and sticks to a nesting spot up high.

The common tailorbirds are named for their clever sewing skills. These birds stitch leaves together to create their home.

Common Tailorbird

Baya Weaver

Ruby-throated
Hummingbird

Mistle Thrush

Bald Eagle

BLOSSOMS

See the blossom, dancing down! Frosting branches, coating ground, turning pavements pink all over the world.

Say, *Hello!*

Bonjour!

Konnichiwa!

to spring.

A blossom is a flower that grows on plants, often used to refer to the flowers of fruit trees, such as oranges, cherries, apples and almonds.

Cherry blossoms are Japan's national flower and they have gifted cherry trees to countries all around the world, such as the US, South Korea and France.

Cherry trees only flower for a week or two. Because they bloom for such a short time, Japan has a traditional custom called *Hanami*, which means "flower viewing". To make the most of the beautiful flowers friends often meet to share food beneath the blooming cherry trees.

SPRING BLOOMS

· ·

Who has seen a flower open; unfold its face to the Sun? You can sit and watch a bud all day, see nothing. But, turn away to play, to sleep, and the petals will dance into being!

Floriography is the language of flowers. A red tulip says, "I love you". A purple tulip tells someone they're a good friend, whereas a white tulip says, "I'm sorry".

Daffodils bring a bold yellow splash of colour to spring. What better way to show someone you care by gifting a daffodil to someone special? The flowers are thought to bring a person happiness.

The bright funnel-shaped blooms of the crocus are one of the first spring flowers you might notice. Some grow in high alpine regions, so don't mind a bit of snow.

· ·

BLUEBELL WOODS

. . . .

When you stumble upon bluebells, it feels like magic; a blue ocean lapping the trunks of tall trees. Skid to a halt and let your mind set sail… you don't see this every day.

According to old folk tales, bluebells ring at daybreak to call fairies to the woods. Sometimes called "fairy flowers", bluebells are said to have been used by fairies to lure and trap people passing by.

About half the world's bluebell population is found in the the UK. Once planted bluebell seeds take around five years to grow into a bulb – when a bluebell has taken root they are one of the first flowers to bloom in springtime.

Many insect species feed on bluebells. Some bees drink bluebell nectar by nipping a small hole in the flower. Ants feed on bluebell seeds, which helps to spread them far and wide.

Bluebells have even been used by humans. Gum from the sap of bluebells was once used as glue to bind the pages of books and to glue feathers onto arrows.

. . . .

DANDELION SEEDS

It takes but a sigh for a dandelion seed to set sail, floating on the lightest breeze. No plans, they go where the wind takes them. Until they fall, trust the soil, wait to grow, and accept change.

The tiny threads on a dandelion seed create a whirlwind that help it to fly. Each tiny seed can travel up to 62 miles (100 km) – that would take a person days and days to walk.

The wind flies these dandelion seeds to new places. When they land the seeds plant themselves in the earth and start to sprout shoots of new dandelion plants, in a process known as germination. Soon, the seeds from these plants will be whisked away somewhere far away to begin this jouney all over again.

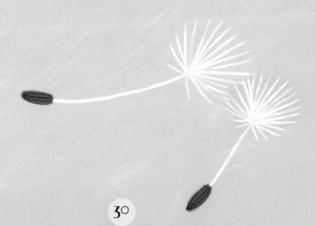

Watermelon

Cherry

Sunflower

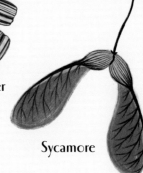
Sycamore

Eucalyptus

SEEDS

· ·

Uncarina

Colourful, tasty, winged, spiky; seeds find their way. On clothes, the wind, through bodies, the ocean, they hold life tight. Have you held one in the palm of your hand? You can almost feel its tiny beating heart. Plant it in the earth, add sun and water, and this little life will start to grow.

A seed no bigger than a pinhead can grow into the tallest plant on the planet. But before they can grow tall and strong seeds need to find the perfect place to lay down their roots. Some seeds fly on the wind, travelling thousands of miles across continents until they find the best place to grow. Other seeds travel by water – a coconut can float between islands before taking root in the ground.

Some seeds rely on animals to eat them and drop them in nature's best fertilizer – their dung. A spiky seed attached to clothing or fur travels great distances until it drops to the ground and sets down its roots. But, no matter how each seed travels to different places, this is only the start of their story.

· ·

Pine Nut

Pomegranate

Pumpkin

Pistachio

Cress

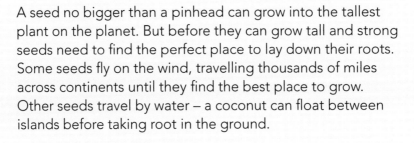

Grape

Pea

Avocado

Coconut

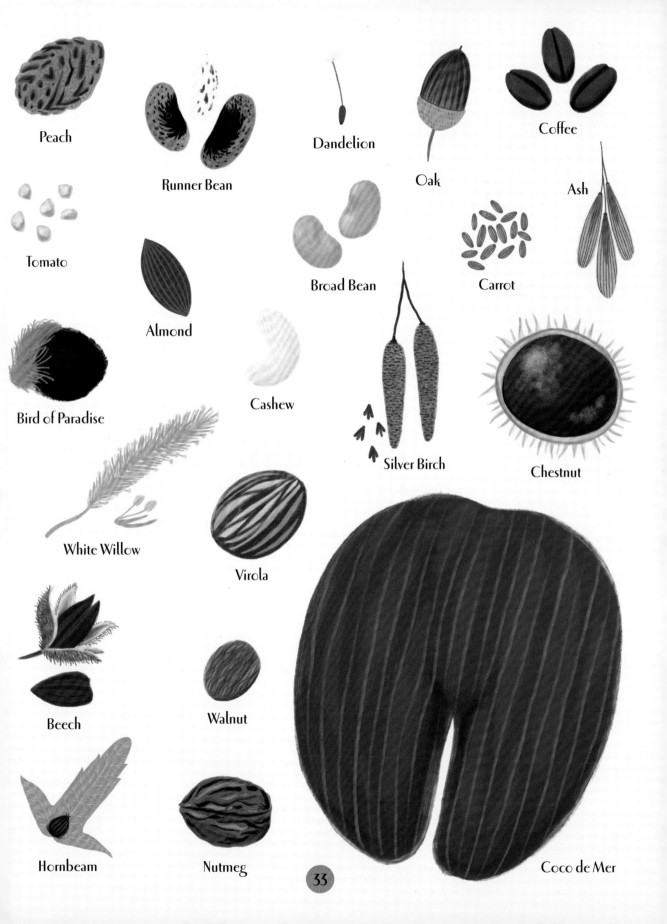

Peach

Runner Bean

Dandelion

Oak

Coffee

Tomato

Almond

Broad Bean

Carrot

Ash

Bird of Paradise

Cashew

Silver Birch

Chestnut

White Willow

Virola

Beech

Walnut

Coco de Mer

Hornbeam

Nutmeg

33

WETLANDS

Geese hissing, honking. Ducks splashing, quacking. Heron standing, still. They see bubbles rising from a diving duck; wet pearls glistening on a goose's back. Do you see them? Watching, waiting, standing, still?

If you see bubbles on the water, keep watching – it could be a duck diving for food. They'll soon swim back up to the surface as good as new, thanks to their protective outer layer of feathers. Ducks often use their bill to spread a layer of oil – released from a gland near their tail – onto their feathers, making them waterproof. Beneath this layer lies another layer of soft feathers called down, which keep a duck warm.

Herons live in heronries of up to 500 birds – one tree can hold ten nests. Making their home near water, herons quietly stand at the water's edge waiting to quickly snatch up any fish that swims past.

During much of the year, Canada geese live in large flocks – except when they are nesting with their mate. Unlike many other animals, Canada geese usually find one mate to stay with for life.

FOREVER GREEN

From hedgerow to rainforest, one colour is king. Not the fleeting flower that blooms and falls. There, in the emerald grass, the noble vines, the verdant leaves and the inky pines. It carpets the ground and touches the sky – green, forever green.

Plants are green because of a chemical called chlorophyll, which they use to absorb light from the Sun. Plants take in carbon dioxide and water which using the Sun's energy they convert into oxygen (humans need this to breathe) and sugars, which plants use to grow. This process is known as photosynthesis.

Evergreen trees, such as pine, hold on to their green foliage even through the winter. By contrast deciduous trees, such as maple, lose their leaves every autumn and regrow them in the spring.

Humans can see more shades of green than any other colour. This helped our ancestors to spot any plants that were tasty – or hazardous. Knowing which plants are edible always comes in handy but equally just being in nature is good for you. Being in green spaces has been proven to make us feel calm.

EVERGREEN

Paws scatter beads of morning dew, toes splatter slick river slime, fingers walk the trunk of an ancient tree. Mud oozes, sand runs, compost trickles. The wind lifts hair, a feather, some fur; sets it back down. Every step, every squelch, every tickle, tells us – you're here, you're alive! When you're outside, touching nature, nature touches you.

The best soil for growing plants in is as soft as breadcrumbs – it helps seeds lay down their roots. Once a plant is rooted to the spot it can grow and thrive for countless years – sometimes for centuries! Each year trees experience growth in different ways. As it gets older gnarly oak bark grows thicker every year. Silver birch bark peels off in papery thin curls, making way for new bark to replace the old.

Some plants have been around for millennia! Fan-shaped tickly ferns have been around for 383 million years – making them older than dinosaurs. Squashy moss happens to be among the first land plants that ever grew on Earth, (oh, and it was so absorbent it was used as bandages during the First World War).

LOOK UP: CLOUDS

Make a bed of the grass, a pillow of your hands, and look up at fleecy clouds sailing by. Shape-shifters making pictures, dancing, chasing past the Sun. Look up at the clouds and you'll never be bored again.

Drifting high above and making a breathtaking display each cloud has its own story. Cumulus can grow to be very large and store lots of rain inside them. But if you see grey skies, it's likely to be altostratus covering the Sun.

If you hear people mention "mackerel skies", they're talking about the fishscale patterns of altocumulus or cirrocumulus. Many clouds make their presence known with beautiful shapes, but cirrostratus clouds are so thin they're often invisible.

Often hovering just a few hundred feet above the Earth, cumulonimbus clouds are formed of multiple cloud levels that can stretch high up into the sky.

All water, even water in your bath, will one day become a cloud – water turns into vapour and floats upwards. The vapour turns into water droplets, which float in the air.

Nimbostratus

Cumulonimbus

Cumulus

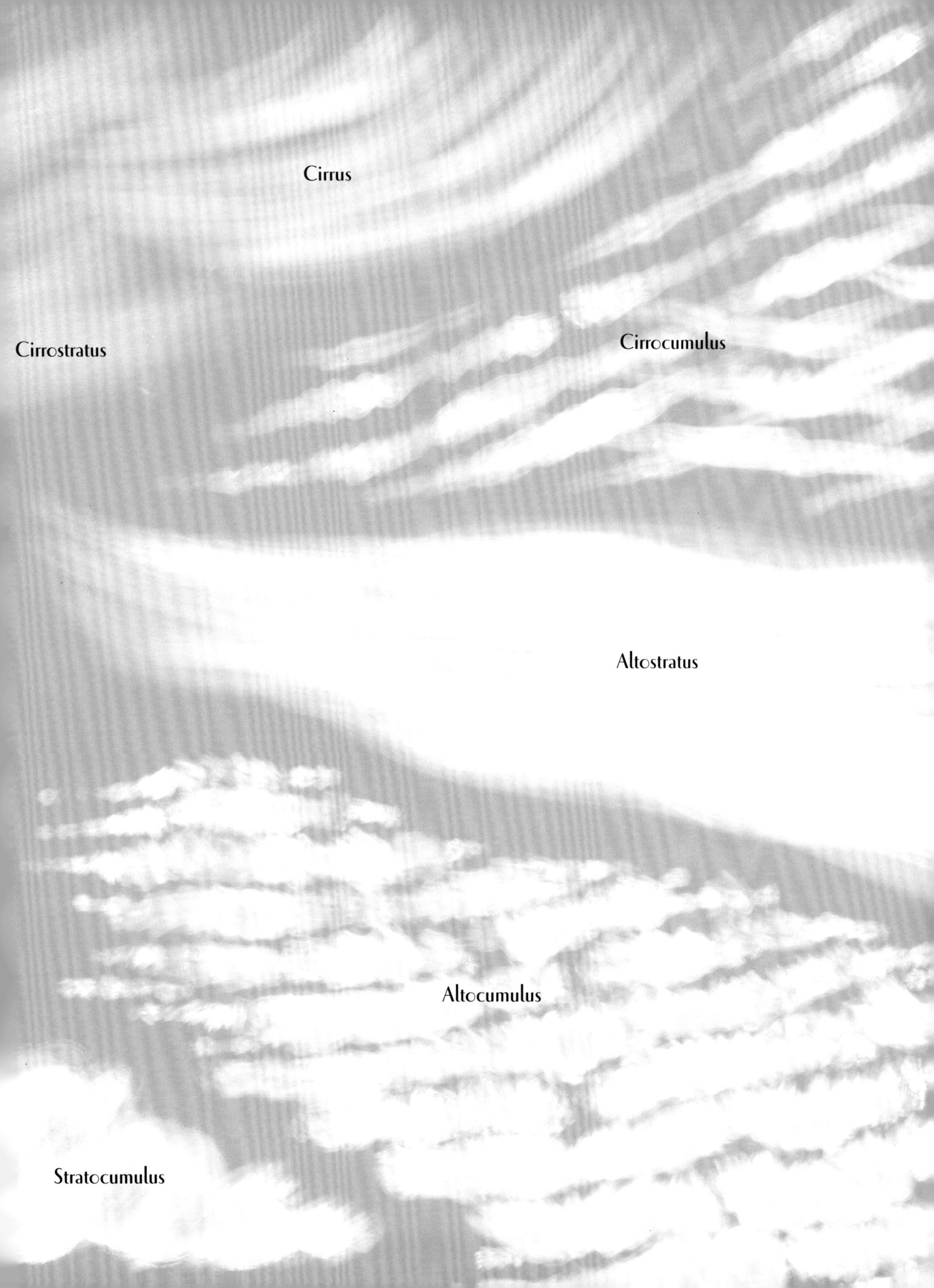

Cirrus

Cirrostratus

Cirrocumulus

Altostratus

Altocumulus

Stratocumulus

SUMMER

SUMMER

After spring comes golden summer, the season of sandy toes, swimming outdoors and ice cream melting down your hand. The Sun has risen to its highest point in the sky, making the days long and warm, so we naturally spend more time outside. We get out our arms and legs, our sunhats and sunscreen, and look for any excuse to be out under a bright blue sky.

This is the season when the world slows down. We associate summer with long, lazy days because there is no school and, often, we go on holiday. There seem to be fewer rules, somehow, and more time to spend with family and friends. Even grown-ups feel this magic in the air in summertime. Summer makes us slower because it is hotter. You can't rush around on a summer's day without needing a big drink and a lie down!

In some tropical parts of the world, heat is a more constant presence and animals and plants have adapted to live in extreme conditions. In this section, you'll travel from garden to desert and rainforest, marvelling at the extremes the powerful Sun can bring. And you'll learn more about the incredible species that inhabit our world.

As for your own adventures, what will you choose? Now is the time for building dens, eating outdoors, sleeping under the stars and making memories with friends that will last a lifetime.

THE SUN

• •

See the Sun rising: turning heads, one-by-one. In a single, sunlit moment, butterfly flutters from flower to flower, meerkat hunts for lunch, and monkey turns to rest. Morning, noon and night flow like a wave across the world. From meadow to rainforest, every living thing gains life from the Sun. The Sun provides the heat and light that enables plants to grow; to ensure day follows night follows day follows night. Can you feel it? The power of our Sun.

Every day, the Sun helps life to thrive on Earth. The Sun's power is a delicate balance; its heat and light can harm us, and in some places it makes it very difficult for new life to grow. In the hot, dry desert, only a few plants and animals have evolved to cope with the Sun's extreme heat.

The Sun is the closest star to Earth. There are thousands of stars like our Sun in the Universe, but Earth is the only place – that we know of – that can support life. The Sun's mass holds the Solar System together, keeping everything, including planet Earth in its orbit.

• •

WILDFLOWERS

Listen to the wildflower patch; humming, warm buzzing, wings thrumming, tissue-paper petals swishing, seeds popping, grasses crackling! This wild patch, rising higher than your knee, fizzes with life and possibilities. Leave a lawn to grow and you'll see different wild flowers and grasses.

Wildflowers provide a haven where bees, butterflies and small animals can live and feed. Sweet-smelling nectar and bright colours attract insects. When insects feed, pollen attaches to their bodies and travels with them from flower to flower. This process enables pollination and is how fertile seeds are produced. Without pollinators (insects such as butterflies and bees which help move pollen between plants) many of the fruit and vegetables we eat would not be produced.

Bird's-Foot Trefoil

Knapweed

Viper's Bugloss

Sainfoin

Ragged Robin

Teasel

Foxglove

Poppy

Meadow Cranesbill

Daisy

Corncockle

PATTERNS ON A BUTTERFLY

Have you stopped to watch a butterfly flutter by? A swirl of colours, dancing from flower to flower. When she lands, she may close her wings. Wait a while, soon the wings will open, spread out like a painting, hovering. Until the butterfly flutters and the patterns are a beautiful blur again.

A butterfly's wings help it to escape predators. Some have wings that are camouflaged when they're closed. Others have markings that look like a large eye to scare birds away. Most people think butterflies have two wings, but look closely and you'll see four – two on each side.

Butterflies love sunny spots with lots of flowers and long grass. If you're hoping to spot a butterfly, choose a warm, calm day. Attract butterflies to your garden by planting nectar-rich flowers, such as buddleja and letting the grass grow long.

Blue Morpho, the Americas

Ringlet, UK and Europe

Anna's Eighty-Eight, the Americas

Red Admiral, UK and Europe

Speckled Wood, UK and Europe

Painted Lady, UK, Africa and Europe

Marine Blue, the Americas

Small Copper, UK and Europe

Peacock, UK and Europe

Alpine Black
Swallowtail, Asia

Peacock Pansy, Asia

Crowned Hairstreak, the Americas

Emerald
Swallowtail,
Southeast Asia

Common Blue, UK and Europe

Swallowtail, UK and Europe

Orange Tip, UK and Europe

Monarch, North America

Gray Hairstreak, the Americas

INDUSTRIOUS INSECTS

No matter what you do, there will always be an insect busier than you. Marching, sawing, lifting, carrying, spinning, inventing: building homes, no, palaces, no, skyscrapers! Ready for their young.

Weaver ants create nests by curving leaves and stitching them together, using the silk produced by their young. A weaver ant's strong jaw can carry objects fifty times their body weight.

Leaf cutter ants' jaws vibrate 1,000 times per second cutting leaves to carry back to their nests. The leaves grow fungus, which the ants feed on. Many ants farm aphids, small plant sap sucking insects, milking them for a sweet substance. In return, the ants protect the aphids from predators, such as ladybirds.

Dung beetles are born into their very own dung sausage – a delicious all-you-can-eat buffet! Dung beetles roll dung to take back to their burrows. But how do you find your way when you're rolling a ball of dung that's bigger than you can see around? You follow the stars.

Termites never sleep. They build colonies twenty-four hours a day, every day of their lives. Termites create huge, clever nests with in-built air-conditioning systems that rival human technology. The combined weight of all the termites in the world would be greater than the total weight of all the humans.

Silk worms are actually moth larvae. They spin luxurious silk into cocoons – an outer casing – which they use to protect themselves while transforming from a caterpillar into an adult moth. Their silk can be used to create fabric.

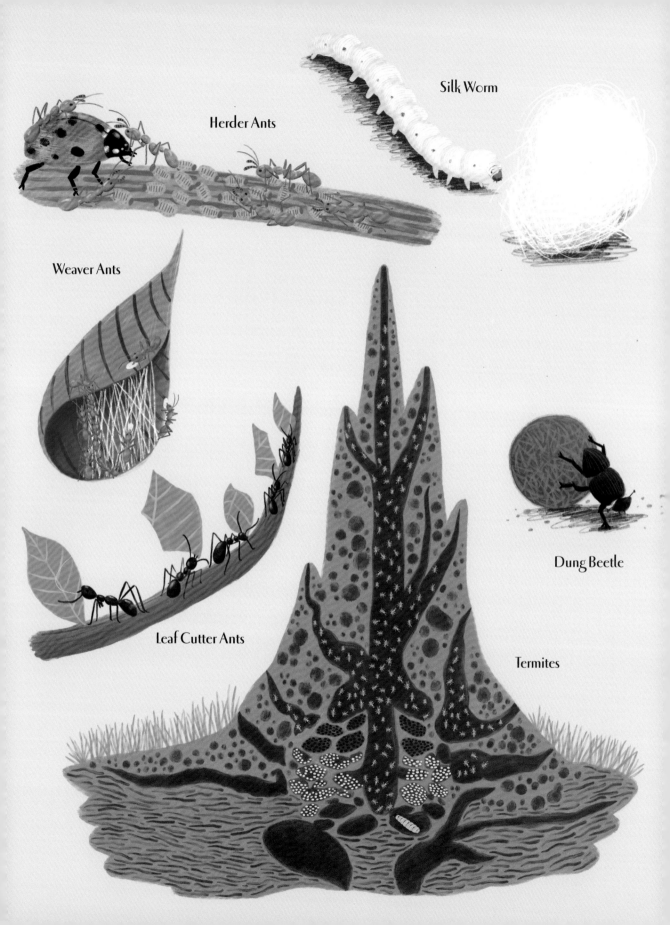

Silk Worm

Herder Ants

Weaver Ants

Dung Beetle

Leaf Cutter Ants

Termites

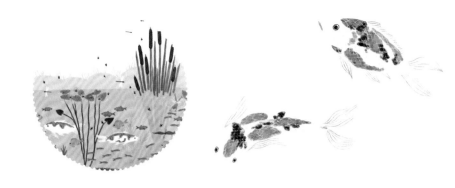

AT THE POND

· ·

What do the fish see, as they slowly swim past? Tadpoles growing legs, leaping on to lily pads. Larvae, crawling upwards, destined to fly. Snails slithering between pond and earth; birds and bees, visitors, coming and going. Are they content, the fish, swimming in silken water, looking up with curious eyes? They seem to be, don't they?

Tadpoles grow back legs first, then front legs and then their tail shrinks. In three months, they become a tiny frog. Some frogs in the world shed their skin in a week. After the old, dead skin is pulled off, it is usually eaten by the frogs. When eating, a frog blinks its big eyes to help push food from its mouth down to its stomach.

Dragonfly larvae hatch in water. When they're ready, they crawl out of the water, shed their hard, outer skin (exoskeleton) and unfold their wings. Dragonflies are expert hunters. They catch prey with their feet, in the air, and hardly ever miss.

· ·

GARDEN SCENTS

The mole doesn't need a torch, the bees don't carry a map, there's no sat-nav guiding fox from den to dell. Invisible highways are travelled by smell alone. We have it, this sense – a whiff of perfume or freshly mown grass can carry the mind, and if we let it; could guide the body home.

Whether we're aware of it or not, the human brain has the ability to navigate by smell. Smell attracts attention, helping plants to be pollinated – or even encouraging animals and people to eat them. When birds and other animals eat plants, it helps them to spread their seeds.

Some people choose plants for their smell: chocolate cosmos with its brownish-red petals and the ridged, narrow leaves of chocolate mint all release a cocoa-like scent. With four small petals on the top and four on the bottom the white-petalled *Nemesia* "Wisley Vanilla", smells just like cake or ice cream.

A sense of smell is important to humans. Over time, humans have evolved to dislike the smell of animal dung to keep us safe from the germs. However, dung is a great fertilizer as it holds nutrients which helps plants to grow.

Sweet Corn

Plum

Blueberry

Lychee

Carrot

FRUITS AND VEGETABLES

Chilli Pepper

Green Pea

You can taste sunshine in raspberries plump from the branch, in the burst of tomato warm on your tongue, in peas popped sweet, straight from the pod. Each fruit steals a little sunlight and holds it tight – until you burst them with your teeth!

We think of cucumbers and tomatoes as vegetables but technically they are types of fruit as they contain seeds inside. There are 10,000 varieties of tomato in the world.

Strawberry

Made of 92 per cent water, watermelons can grow to be extremely large. The largest watermelon ever grown weighed 159 kg. It filled the back of a truck.

Potato

Native to South America, the pineapple got its name from European explorers who named the fruit after its resemblance to a pine cone. But in many countries the fruit is still called by its original name, *ananas*. The name was given to the fruit by the Tupi people and supposedly means "excellent fruit".

Broccoli

Mango

Cucumber

Watermelon

Raspberry

Carambola

Courgette

Melon

Durian

Lemon

Aubergine

Lettuce

Tomato

Pineapple

Cherry

Grape

Banana

Bell Pepper

Broad Bean

INSIDE A HIVE

Listen for the sweet buzz of honey bees; watch them fly from flower to flower, bodies flecked with pollen. They are lost in the heady task of collecting nectar. Somewhere, combs await in a hive, filled with the honeyed hum of a thousand bees who live to serve their queen. How lost we'd be without bees.

By flying from flower to flower, bees and other insects pollinate many plants, from coffee plants in Brazil to apple trees in Britain. Worker bees are always female and they are very important to keeping a hive healthy. They don't just collect pollen and nectar to turn into honey, they do all the work in the hive too. They build and protect the hive, feed the grubs and tend the queen.

A queen bee's job is to lay eggs, which will become the next generation of bees. The queen also produces chemicals that affect the behaviour of other bees, which helps keep all the bees working together in harmony.

COLOURFUL BIRDS

The flight of birds lifts eyes to the skies; a flash of red or blue or gold makes hearts flutter; morning to evening connects us to the day. The males are the stage-stealers, tail shakers, brightly plumed dancers; the females, experts of camouflage, wait to be impressed. They are harder to please than us.

Birds have a unique y-shaped voice box which some use to create beautiful songs. Male birds use songs and their bold colouring to attract a mate. In contrast many female birds often have feathers that help them blend into the landscape and protect themselves and their young.

Their bright feathers are attention-grabbing but birds have other features that are just as fascinating. The toucan's colourful beak has blood vessels in it that radiate heat, helping it to cool down or warm up.

A scarlet macaw's strong beak can tear open unripe fruit and help it to climb. They often use their left claw to pick up objects, while their right leg helps to support their body.

A bee hummingbird rarely grows bigger than six centimetres. Yet they can beat their wings eighty times per second, and can fly straight up, backwards and even upside down.

Blue jays feast on ants, which they rub on their feathers before they eat them. No one knows the exact reason why. Scientists say the ants might release something that helps to protect the birds.

On the opposite page are some bird species from different parts of the world. Not all of these birds are native to every country, why not check out which country you might see each species in?

Toucan

Flame Robin

Kingfisher

Greenfinch

Blue Tit

Fire-Tufted Barbet

Guianan Cock-of-the-Rock

Scarlet Macaw

Red-Backed Fairy-Wren

Eurasian Bullfinch

Bee Hummingbird

Long-Tailed Manakin

Wine Throated Hummingbird

Wilson's Bird of Paradise

Curl-Crested Aracari

Blue Jay

Flame Bowerbird

Royal Flycatcher

Goldfinch

Mallard

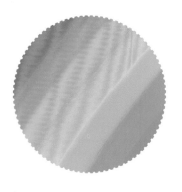

RAINBOW

· ·

When you notice a rainbow, do you wonder how long it's been waiting, with an upside-down grin, for you to smile back at it? Sometimes you see escapees hovering over waterfalls, bouncing off a jewelled finger, landing on a wall. We know the colours, the science but, in the moment, all that matters is the magic that suspends life until the colours dissolve.

"Rainbow" comes from the latin *arcus pluvius*, meaning "rainy arch". Each person sees a rainbow differently, depending on where they are standing. And different people see different colours in a rainbow.

Isaac Newton was a scientist and pioneer in research on light. He loved to put plain sunlight through prisms and watch it change colour. He set out the colours of the rainbow in an order schoolchildren still memorize today: red, orange, yellow, green, blue, indigo and violet.

For a rainbow to appear, the Sun needs to be behind you and sitting low in the sky. René Descartes, a scientist, discovered rainbows appear when lightwaves from the Sun are split by water droplets in rain. The same can occur when light hits a mist, a waterfall or even a glass of water.

· ·

THE SEA

The sea can be crazy, calm or cross, but the sea I love best is playful, with waves that bob and surge and dance, lift up surfer, seagull, both, and rush them to shore. Some seas tease, they creep up until you see your sand sculptures dissolving in foam; other times, they slip away, leaving an ocean of sand between the waves and your toes. The angry sea is thrilling, with crashing waves that tower, rooting feet firmly to land. But the cheerful sea invites you in – to play and splash and swim.

Our planet's oceans cover more than two thirds of the Earth's surface; the Pacific Ocean alone covers one third. The name Pacific Ocean comes from the Latin phrase *tepre pacificum*, which means "peaceful sea".

The Earth's seas are so vast that an entire mountain range could be found beneath the water. In fact, one such mountain range exists! The mid-ocean ridge is the longest mountain range in the world and it stretches below the sea from the Arctic Ocean through the Atlantic Ocean and round the southern tip of Africa.

The gravitational pull of the Sun and Moon on the Earth causes the tides, while wind causes most of the waves we see coming in from the horizon. Waves carry energy, which surfers (and seagulls) can ride on. This energy can be turned into clean energy – in fact, the world's first wave power farm was created in Portugal.

Sundial

Cameo Helmet

Paper Nautilus

SHELLS

· ·

The sea brings gifts: a fan, a spiral, a unicorn horn, and she pops them on the sand. "Lift this one," she says, "and it'll sing you a song." You hear the sea, a distant storm, and then something else – the trace of a memory, of life clung tightly inside the twisted walls. Molluscs and mussels, scallops and snails, a whole life is lived inside a shell.

Tusk

Spun in tight circles or clammed shut, shells are home to a variety of life. A precious pearl is created when an irritant, such as a small parasite burrows inside an oyster. The oyster protects itself by coating the intruder with layer upon layer of nacre, which is also known as mother of pearl. After many years, a smooth, shiny pearl forms.

Abalone

Episcopal
Miter

Shells grow with the creatures that live inside them. Some grow in ever increasing spirals – the tip at the very centre is the shell the creature was born with, before it began to expand. When the creature dies, its shell can wash up on the shore. And, though, the shell has found its way ashore, a remnant of the sea remains still. Lift a spiral conch shell to your ear and you'll hear a sound that's like the rush of the sea.

Blue Mussel

· ·

Junonia

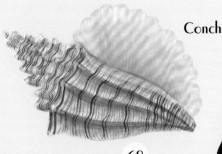
Conch

Razor Clam

Trochidae

Auger

Cowrie

Sand Dollar

Urchin

Starfish

Oyster

Scotch Bonnet

Whelk

Limpet

Horse Conch

Periwinkle

Barnacle

Cockle

Violet Snail

Queen Helmet

Baby's Ear

Cone Shell

Scallop

A STORM

• •

The thrill of the summer storm starts with bruised sky, brooding. Feeling of foreboding, building, until lightning breaks the dam. A distant rumble rises to a roar, rain slaps the ground, rattles gutters, and trees give voice to angry wind. You, with your nose pressed close to the glass, you count. Is the fury getting closer or further away?

Thunderstorms occur more often when there is moisture or warm air in the atmosphere, which is why storms thrive in summertime. Storms help plants flourish too. Lightning helps fertilize the soil, the massive amounts of electrical energy converts nitrogen in the air into a form that plants can absorb from the soil.

A bolt of lightning is as slender as a thumb and five times hotter than the Sun. When lightning strikes sand, it can fuse together the grains of sand into a small, glass-like tube known as a fulgurite.

• •

INTO THE RAINFOREST

In the raucous rainforest, one animal is silent, with near-blind eyes and a sleepy smile. But don't be fooled. He may be slow, but sloth senses it all. He smells bark peeling from a tree, seedlings sprouting in fertile soil, fresh rain washing scents from here to there. He hears toucans croak, frogs bark, monkeys shriek – their din ricocheting off the high canopy. And all the time, sloth is silent, eyes blinking slowly, taking it all in.

Sloths are strong. They can lift their entire body weight with one arm. They are almost blind but they have a phenomenal memory of locations and sense of smell, which helps them navigate through the rainforest.

Tropical rainforests are some of the noisiest places on Earth – a howler monkey's call can be heard three miles away. Rainforests are found in the tropics of Central and South America, Western and Central Africa, Western India, Southeast Asia and Australia. Tropical rainforests are found close to the Equator. Because the weather is warm the air found in rainforests is always hot and steamy.

Most rainforests have four layers: emergent, canopy, understory and forest floor. As the topmost layer, the emergent layer receives the most sunlight and rain. The canopy is the next layer and because so much food is available more animals live in this layer than any other. The understory provides shelter for small animals and birds that live in the trees. The forest floor is the lowest layer. Only two per cent of sunlight reaches this layer so it is always dark, hot and damp. Heavy rain falls most days and drips constantly from the canopy to the forest floor.

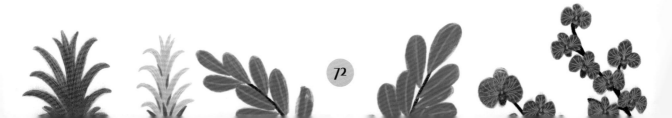

REFLECTIONS IN A RAINDROP

Do you think the raindrop on the cloud feels anticipation? Looking down, waiting for his turn to free fall! Sky dive – once in a lifetime thrill ride! Is he destined for puddle, gutter, river or umbrella? Or will he form a perfect pearl, suspended from a branch, waiting, again, for his turn to drop! To soak the soil, provide a drink for root, mole or worm. And then, wait. For, one day, this little raindrop will rise again.

Rainforests aren't the only place where it rains, the water cycle can lead to rain in many other places on Earth. As water rises, it evaporates into water vapour, which condenses into clouds. The water droplets in the cloud grow until they're too heavy and then they fall as rain. Rain enters the ground, the rivers and the sea. All water on Earth is part of this delicate cycle, and it connects us all – the water you use to wash your hair could one day fall on a garden in Australia.

Every plant and animal on Earth needs water to survive. It's important we restore the balance to keep our planet and all who live on it safe. Humans are upsetting the delicate balance of the water cycle by using more water than we need.

A DESERT GARDEN

· ·

The cactus doesn't wilt. The fox doesn't hop, foot to foot, across burning sand. They thrive, where we would struggle to stay alive! Solitary types – even the plants grow spikes. But, beneath the thorns, there's a peaceful existence in harmony with the barren land; these creatures couldn't live anywhere but here.

The fennec fox has adapted to live without drinking water, obtaining most of its water from its food. Fennec foxes have very large ears, all the better to hear – and hunt down – their prey with.

Aloe vera sap helps to soothe burnt skin – it is the perfect companion to the Sun. The *Mammillaria hahniana* is better known as the "old lady" cactus because of its grey hairs. There's an "old man" cactus, too (the *Cephalocereus senilis*).

Deserts are arid and dry with very little rainfall. The largest hot desert on Earth is the Sahara Desert in Africa. Animals in the Sahara feast on the wild thyme bushes that grow there. Deserts might make you imagine sand and heat but they can get very cold at night. There are also cold deserts, such as Antarctica.

· ·

AUTUMN

AUTUMN

After summer comes fiery autumn, burning with colour. Look up and you'll see trees blazing red, copper and gold. Soon, the wind will pick them up and carry them to the ground, where they'll create a thick carpet for you to kick through.

At this time of year, animals are busier again, getting ready for winter. Squirrels run from tree to tree collecting acorns to store underground and eat later in the year. Some of the buried acorns will take root and grow into huge oak trees. Birds start to behave differently, too, feeding and some flying restlessly, ready for their next migration.

In these pages, you'll find adventure in the wild elements of wind and rain. You'll learn to identify trees by their leaves and lift rocks to see the tiny creatures that live beneath them. And you'll discover the secrets hidden inside trees.

It's the season for layering up, wearing wellies for walks, for bonfire parties and pumpkins – make sure you try one roasted or in a pie, as they're not just for spooking.

AUTUMN LEAVES

Autumn is coming! The evergreens may not realize, but the sycamores do! Tossing a thousand golden leaves into the sky, autumn leaves don't drop – they fly! Seizing their chance to soar, swirling, sailing, fluttering, dallying, until their time to fall.

Autumn is called "fall" around the world – because leaves fall from the trees. Autumn sheds light on the difference between evergreens and deciduous trees: evergreens, like pines, usually stay green all year; deciduous trees flash golden leaves before shedding them all.

Trees feed on sunlight, this is one reason some drop their leaves, as it helps them to save energy for the cold winter. Chlorophyll makes leaves green. When a plant reabsorbs it in autumn, the leaves change colour.

Equinox means "equal night" – marking the time of the year when night and day are the same length. After the autumn equinox, nights are longer than days.

SPIDER WEBS

Look at the spider: spinner, pattern weaver, casting webs with threads of steel. They wait, in a necklace hung with pearls, for the gentle thrum that tells him: it's dinnertime.

Autumn's mists and dews reveal spiderwebs, which are usually virtually invisible. Some spiders spin webs that are large enough to stretch across entire rivers. A new web can take about two hours to build.

There are different types of webs, from orb (circular) webs to sheet webs, which hang like hammocks in bushes. To create an orb web, a spider drifts a silk thread across a gap and then adds supporting links. Next, they add the radial threads (like the hands of a clock) and then they add the spirals. They finish by removing knots from the centre and replace them with a lattice.

Spider silk is liquid, which hardens when it comes into contact with the air. Their silk is strong – its five times stronger than a strand of steel of the same thickness.

The silk is used by spiders for a number of tasks. They use them as drag lines – attaching them to an object to stop them falling; and ballooning – the threads pick up air currents and can help spiders travel for hundreds of miles.

HARVEST

The autumn garden is full of shining jewels, heavy treasures! Pumpkins pinning vines to the soil, apples stooping trees, brambles bent low by their bounty. These are autumn's riches, winking in the hedgerow, telling us it's time to line our stomachs for winter.

People wonder why brambles produce both thorns and delicious fruit. One guess is this makes the fruit most available to the animals who will spread the seeds further. For this reason, birds are the most desirable feasters.

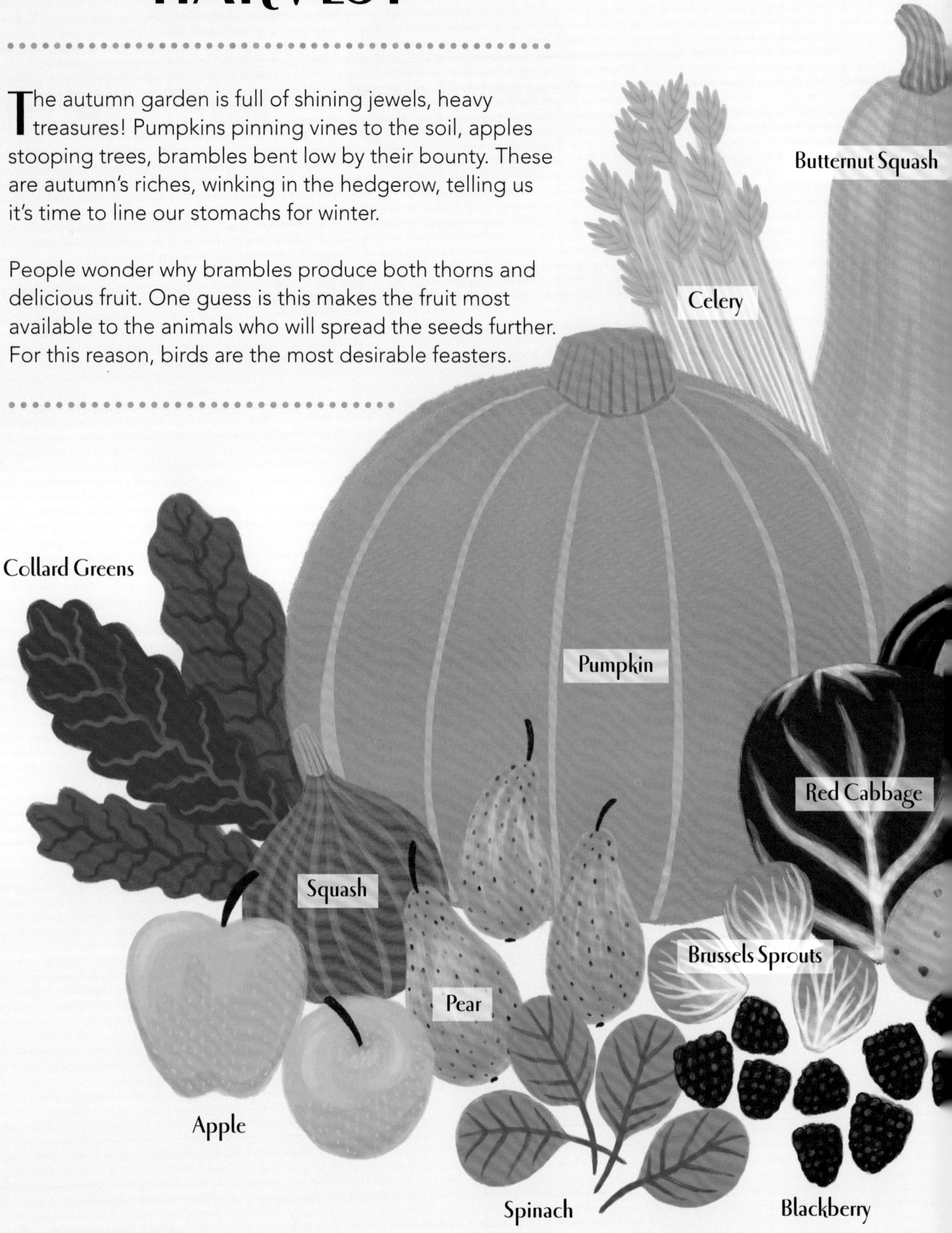

Butternut Squash

Celery

Collard Greens

Pumpkin

Red Cabbage

Squash

Brussels Sprouts

Pear

Apple

Spinach

Blackberry

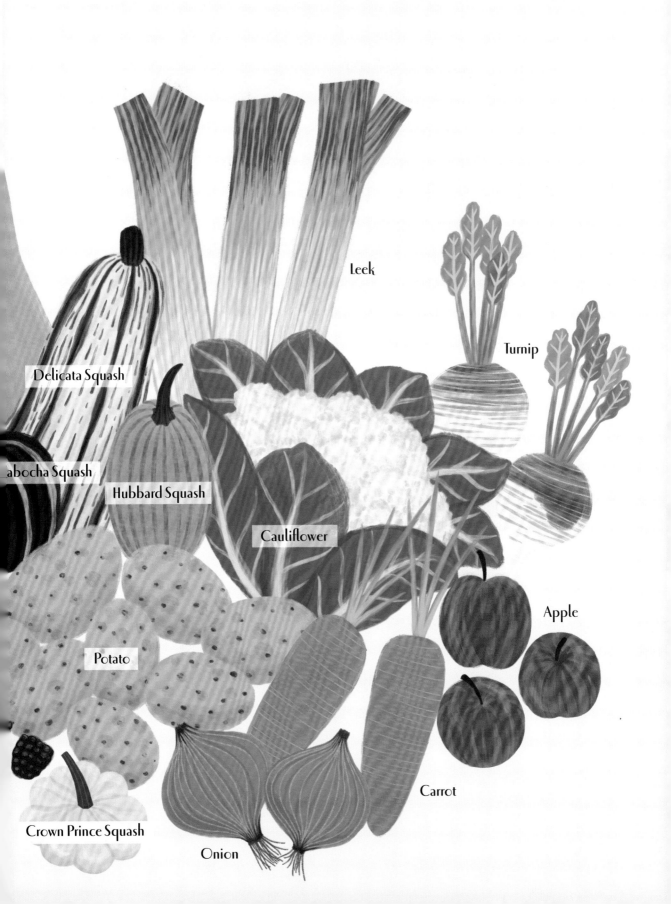

Leek

Turnip

Delicata Squash

abocha Squash

Hubbard Squash

Cauliflower

Apple

Potato

Carrot

Crown Prince Squash

Onion

THE ACORN AND THE OAK TREE

It's hard to believe – impossible, really, that the acorn you hold between finger and thumb may one day grow into a tree, so large it could hold you in its branches; and if you hugged its trunk, stretched your arms as wide as they will go, let bark leave marks upon your cheek, you'd never get your hands to meet. Yes, it's hard to believe but it's true.

Acorns are the seeds of oak trees. Forgotten seeds lie in the soil for weeks, months or even years. And then they start to grow. When there is enough warmth and water, the seed sprouts roots and a shoot, which travels up towards the sky.

When the first tiny, bumpy leaf unfolds, the plant is called a seedling. This tiny plant could be flattened by rain or wind or eaten by an animal. If the seedling survives, it will grow into a sapling – it will look like a small oak tree, but much thinner and smaller. Over time, the sapling will become a young oak tree. This tree will continue to grow upwards and outwards and could live for hundreds of years.

A ROCK GARDEN

. . . .

Look at those bibble-bugs, chisel-hogs, chuggy-pigs, roly-polies, monkey-peas – look at them scurrying! Sprinting from the Sun's glare, hurrying from your stare. Put the rock back down, quick!

Birds who feed on woodlice and other creatures know where they hide, and they have a clever way of coaxing them out: they tap their beak to make it sound like it's raining.

You'll find woodlice under rocks and plant pots, along with beetles, slugs, snails and toads. Woodlice have had many funny nicknames through history. A lot of the names compare them to pigs, due to the bad smell they give out when they release ammonia, a type of gas, from under their skin. A woodlice's shell is like armour as it protects them.

Violet ground beetles are nocturnal creatures, they rest under logs or stones during the day and are active at night. They can't fly, but are fast runners which helps them capture and feed on slugs.

. . . .

DOWNPOUR

Bow to the rain, curtsey if you like, but don't duck undercover. It's not so fun with knuckles white on inside-out umbrella. What if you just decided to get wet? Let it soak your grin, got lost in the plinkety-plink of raindrops splashing, sloshety-sloshing, in puddles pattering, washing your worries clean away.

Water is constantly moving above and below the surface of the Earth, this is known as the water cycle. Precipitation is a stage of the water cycle – it is any type of water that forms in the atmosphere and drops onto the Earth's surface.

Rain forms when warm, wet air rises, then cools to form clouds. The clouds release rain. Rain is the name given to drops that are larger then half a centimetre. Drizzle is made of smaller drops that will cling to your eyelashes. Fog is made of even smaller drops that just sit in the air.

Hail forms in cold storm clouds. They are made of bigger pieces of ice, or snowballs, that clatter out of the sky. About the size of small rocks, hailstones can get as large as fifteen centimetres. Sleet is made of liquid that forms and freezes as it falls to Earth. It's ice, not snow.

HIDDEN HOMES

N‌ext time you're outside, spare a thought for the neighbours underground, in the darkness of the earth. There, a scritch-scratch of giant paws is followed by a burrowing nose. Down here, mole has all his heart desires. Space to dig, time to dig – and earthworms! Plenty of earthworms. Gardeners are not keen on moles: "Pesky animals, leaving mounds of soil on my lawn." But earthworms they tolerate gladly, these up-and-down excavators are the secret ingredient making every garden grow.

Moles are perfectly suited to living underground – their velvety black fur helps them to blend in with the earth. Their tiny eyes can see only light and movement, but this and their sense of smell and touch is enough for them to navigate by. Their spade-like front paws help them to dig, dig, dig.

Moles create small hills of earth when they first tunnel underground. After that they disappear and spend their time digging tunnels and rooms. Moles are shy creatures. They sense vibrations and if anyone or anything approaches, they dive back underground.

Moles share the soil with earthworms – their favourite meal. Worms are more important than you think: they pull dead plant materials down into the soil, providing nutrients for new plants to grow. A worms' wriggling and burrowing adds air to the soil and helps water drain away. Worms also provide a meal for foxes, hedgehogs, frogs and toads.

ROCKS AND FOSSILS

The rocks are breathing – sleeping giants, filled with secrets. Fossils! Creatures frozen in time. Until a root finds a crack or water pounds a cliff and the stories come tumbling out. Another type of rock arrives in a ball of light, streaks the sky with tales from space. There's magic in both of them. Which do you prefer?

Rocks can be beautiful. Look closely and you'll see many colours and textures. These rocks may have fossils inside to tell you what creatures once lived there. Amber is formed when prehistoric tree resin is preserved into a soft rock – sometimes with insects or small mammals inside.

Heat, pressure or often both cause igneous or sedimentary rocks to turn into metamorphic rocks. Shiny marble, grey slate and pink skarn are metamorphic rocks. Some rocks hold metals inside them, such as gold, silver or iron.

Sedimentary rocks are made of squished together sediments – small pieces of plants, animals, salt or other chemicals. They often form distinctive layers.

Igneous rocks form when boiling hot magma (molten rock) cools and becomes solid. Basalt rock tells you lava from a volcano once flowed over the land. Meteorites are rocks from space. Most of them are broken asteroids, which orbit the Sun.

Pink Granite

Tektites

Copper

Sandstone

Pele's Hair

Fulgurite

Chalk

Flint

Amber

Gneiss

Conglomerate

Gold

Obsidian

Marble

Ammonite

THE WIND

A utumn's wind is fun-loving, ruffles hair and combs grass, lifts the gaze to singing branches. Yes, spring wind is fresh, blows away the cobwebs. Summer breeze is sweet, a welcome retreat. Winter gale steals your breath, takes it somewhere new. But autumn's gusts choreograph a thousand glowing leaves, blows you on to join them in their dance between the trees.

Wind is air in motion, created by the Sun's uneven heating of the Earth's surface. A gust of wind is a short, powerful blast. A breeze is more gentle than a gust, and can be called a zephyr. A sirocco is a hot, desert wind. A haboob is a violent dust or sandstorm. A squall is sudden, violent and often brings rain or snow. A gale refers to a current of air that measures up to sixty miles per hour (ninety-six kilometres) – it's fiercer than a gust of wind.

LEAF SHAPES

Poplar

Beech

This is the secret of how to read trees – study the leaves! Not in a book (although it helps), but, there, on the tree, on the ground, on the sapling. Touch the fingers, count the lobes, and soon they'll appear as old friends.

Some trees grow lots of leaves on one leaf stalk. These leaves are called leaflets. The long sections of horse chestnut and sycamore leaves are called fingers. Oak and hawthorn have waves on their leaves, called lobes (like an earlobe). Look for veins: these carry water and food through the leaves.

Leaves come in all shapes and sizes, but they play a very important role for a plant's health. Leaves are the main parts of the plant that captures sunlight and convert it to energy, which a plant uses to grow. Most plants have wide and flat leaves, but plants in difficult habitats have adapted to survive. Plants found in a rainforest need big leaves to catch as much sunlight as possible in the crowded space. Cliffside plants get plenty of sunlight but have small, strong leaves to survive the powerful wind.

Elder

Yew

Ash

Alder

Ivy

Sycamore

Apple

Elm

Cherry

Willow

Hawthorn

Hazel

Oak

Birch

Aspen

Maple

Rowan

TALKING TREES

Did you know, a felled tree is like an open book? The story of its life, written into the rings of its trunk. In the woods, there's shrieking, chirruping, shouting and barking, but it is the silent tree who speaks to us, telling tales of years gone by. It says, "A fire, a feast, a thirsty year, look closely at my rings. I'm older than your great-grandfather, let me tell you the things I have seen."

How old is this tree? Most trees live for over a hundred years. You can tell how old a tree is by counting its rings. Tree trunks grow thicker every year by adding a new ring of growth.

If a tree has plenty of water and light, it grows quickly so the ring is thick. If there is a shortage of water, the tree grows slowly and the ring is thinner. Fire, lightning or even frost can hurt a tree, leaving little clues in the rings.

What else might the tree have seen in its lifetime? Wildlife, planes, sports, children playing, buildings being made – what else can you think of?

102

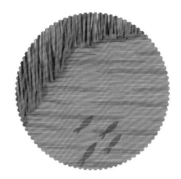

BIRD'S EYE VIEW

What's it like up there? Looking down with telescopic eyes. Do ospreys see only prey, or do they lie on a wave that laps the clouds and gaze at glinting water? Do they look at toy sheep and lollipop trees, at cars that move like glinting beetles? Do they see us and wonder what it's like down here, looking up at them?

Ospreys glide on wind currents, like waves of air in the sky. Ospreys travel at the speed of a car, accelerating from thirty – fifty miles per hour (forty-eight – eighty kilometres) when they hit the water.

They fly about seventy metres above the water's surface to search for their prey, which include fish, such as salmon and trout. Once they catch sight of their prey they dive downward with their wings half-folded to catch it.

A pair of ospreys usually mate for life and lay between one to three eggs per season. It takes up to forty-two days for the eggs to hatch. A chick learns how to fly about two months after hatching; it stays in the nest for another two months while it learns how to fish.

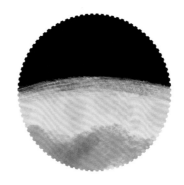

THE MOON

• •

Look at the Moon, full tonight, pooling light like candle wax. Time shifts, and as the Moon, Earth and Sun dance their orbital dance, a grain of light trickles away. Look at the Moon, waning tonight. As sure as night follows day it will shrink to a crescent, and disappear before it's born again.

The Moon orbits Earth. It doesn't give off any light of it's own, but reflects light from nearby planetary bodies. Most of the light comes from the Sun; a small amount of light also comes from distant stars and the Earth – this light is called Earthshine. Depending on the amount of light it gets the Moon seems to change shape, leading to different phases of the moon. It takes the Moon 29.5 days to move through the different phases, from new moon all the way through to waning crescent.

• •

There are eight main phases of the moon:

New moon – in orbit between the Earth and Sun, the side of the Moon facing the Sun is lit up but the side facing Earth is in darkness.

Waxing crescent – the Moon seems to grow or "wax" as the illuminated surface increases.

First quarter – orbiting about a quarter of the way around the Earth, the Moon is equally lit by sunlight and shrouded in darkness.

Waxing gibbous – the Moon is more than half full, and still growing.

Full moon – halfway through it's orbit, the Moon is now on the far side of the Earth and directly opposite to the Sun. With plenty of light the face is fully illuminated.

Waning gibbous – more than half of the surface is lit, but the area is shrinking, or "waning".

Last quarter – half-lit and half-shadowed, this moon rises at midnight and is at its highest peak in the sky around sunrise.

Waning crescent – less than a quarter of the moon is lit as it almost completes its orbit around the Earth.

WINTER

WINTER

After autumn comes winter. You know it's approaching when a bitter wind sends you burrowing inside your coat. One by one, plants shrink to their roots. The Sun shines cold and the nights come early.

One morning, you may wake to a brighter-than-white light and to a thick silence. You know, even before you open the curtain, you'll be greeted by a blanket of snow. Out come toboggans and rosy cheeks. Snowflakes settle on hats and coats as boots squeak and fingers burn in ice-studded gloves.

Once the white shrinks to patches and the snowman's carrot has dropped, it's tempting to close the door and slink away to the sofa. Who can blame you? Some animals disappear altogether in winter. Some birds migrate to hotter lands. The tiniest dormouse and the largest bear make cosy dens to sleep out the season. But, winter has more magic in store, if you know where to look for it.

In this section, you'll discover a thousand birds who dance in a single swirling motion and you'll see the unique patterns in snowflakes. You'll explore beneath the icy crust of a frozen pond and stay up to discover the night sky.

Don't forget to step outside for your own encounters with nature. You can play detective and see which animals have left tracks in the snow, leave food for robins and groups of great tits who will meet regularly in your tree. And a visit to the wildlife at your local river will always make the dullest of days feel full.

SNOWFLAKES

● ●

Did you know, each snowflake is unique? Six-pointed stars, shaped by the sky, and at the heart of each flake, locked inside a crystal, is a single mote of dust. Dust! So now you know. As the grey signet changes into a swan, each snowflake starts life as a speck of grey, which grows wings and glides to earth like a feathered gift from the sky.

A snowflake forms when a drop of water freezes around a tiny particle of dust or pollen. You can see the dust at its heart through a strong microscope.

This tiny ice crystal falls, collecting more crystals of water. Each snowflake combines hundreds of ice crystals in its own unique pattern. The way these crystals join together creates the shape of a snowflake. A snowflake always has six sides or points.

Wilson Bentley was the first person to photograph snowflakes. He said, "Open the skylight, and directly under it place the carefully prepared blackboard, on whose ebony surface the most minute form of frozen beauty may be welcome from cloud-land."

● ●

LOOK UP: STARLINGS!

Quick, look, up there! A swooping cloud, smudging the horizon. A thousand birds billowing, twisting and turning, flowing in a ribbon, tugging all eyes to the sky. Like dancers in a ballet, moving in time. How do they know where to fly?

Starlings flock together in groups called a murmuration. They can fly at speeds of around forty miles per hour (sixty-four kilometres) within a wing's length of each other. It's hard to pick out one bird when the group is moving together. The birds stay together to keep each other safe from predators.

How starlings fly in murmurations has puzzled scientists for a century or more. Telepathic communication was suggested but it is more likely that each bird is following the movement of its neighbours. Everyone can agree, though, the sight of a murmuration of starlings is breathtaking.

WINTER
WOODLAND WALK

· ·

The Sun flashes low through skeleton trees. You step on frost and shadows and twigs that crackle, until – you freeze. For there is a deer. Staring at you, staring at him, waiting, heart-pounding, until suddenly, he disappears. The woods feel different now, touched by magic. Life still beats here.

In winter, the Sun drops low, creating long shadows on the ground. The sky itself often appears white. Large particles of water in the air bounce away all colours – the opposite of a rainbow. Deciduous trees have shed their leaves, and their wooden skeletons are silhouettes against the sky.

Deer do most of their feeding between dusk and dawn, while the world sleeps. But you can search for deer clues. Look for vertical cuts in trees: stags rub the trees to remove the velvet from a new set of antlers, or to mark their scent.

· ·

BENEATH THE ICE

When you look at the pond, ice thick as a book, it's easy to think life has stopped. But the heron knows it's simply on pause – beak poised, she waits for a drowsy frog to breaststroke by, or a goldfish to stir in its bed of reeds. When the ice melts, it won't take long for the dreamers and sleepers to remember how to live. Will they remember the heron?

A heron searches for movement below a hole in the ice, waiting patiently for its prey to swim close to the surface. Under the thick ice on a frozen pond, life slows down but many creatures live there still, waiting for winter to pass.

Water boatman, a type of small aquatic insect, float just below the surface, looking for air bubbles. Like deep sea divers, they have a store of air, they tuck an air bubble under their wings and abdomen.

Koi and goldfish enter a state of dormancy, similar to hibernation. They sit in the warmest water, at the bottom of the pond, lined up neatly so they all fit.

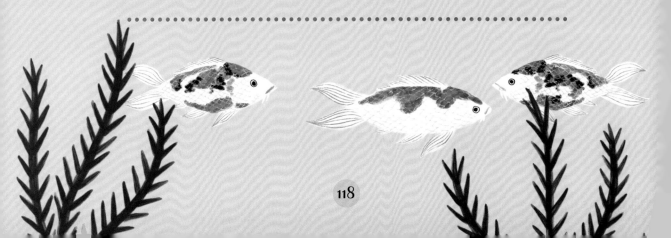

FOOTPRINTS

A fresh sheet of snow may seem like a blank page, but look closer. You'll see creatures have left their mark, writing black against white, tales from last night. Each story is different. Some crept, gave chase, escaped or scuffled. You can see how their story went – and how it ended.

You're likely to see many different footprints have traced the same path in the garden. Look carefully to tell them apart. Rodent tracks show four toes. The heavy step of a bigger bird will sink deeper into the snow. While a fox's footprint looks more like a rounded hole on the surface of the snow.

Large paws find it easier to walk across snow without sinking. You can search for the tracks of a predator following their prey. Look at the direction of the footprints to see which way the creature went.

SUNSET

· ·

See the sun setting, turning clouds pink, streaking sky gold, reminding us tomorrow is a new day. It doesn't matter how many times the burning sun smudges the evening sky, you'll never grow tired of watching it set.

Sunsets are created by a process called scattering. Small particles of water cause sunlight to change direction, which separates the light into different colours.

Cold days produce the most vivid and stunning sunsets. In winter, the Sun sets earlier than at other times of the year and it sits lower in the sky. "Solstice" means "Sun" and "standstill" in Latin because the Sun seems to hover.

· ·

A MIDNIGHT GARDEN

When evening's lights turn on, some animals eat breakfast below the setting Sun. When the lights go out, they live secret lives under star-studded skies. Prowling and howling, hooting and shrieking, swooping without seeing. When you close your eyes, you can hear them: hunting, feasting and playing.

Foxes have a sharp sense of smell to help them navigate in the dark. To fly safely, bats use echolocation, a high-pitched sound that bounces off objects, including their prey.

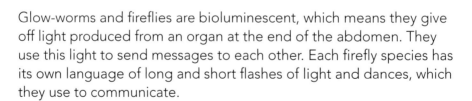

Whiskers are extra sensitive to touch, helping mice and cats to move around safely. Owl eyes are so big they can't move in their socket, but they let in lots of light.

Glow-worms and fireflies are bioluminescent, which means they give off light produced from an organ at the end of the abdomen. They use this light to send messages to each other. Each firefly species has its own language of long and short flashes of light and dances, which they use to communicate.

The dark helps nocturnal animals to hunt or avoid predators. In warmer countries, it makes sense to sleep when the Sun is hot and then to live in the cool of the night. Before you wake, they'll slip away to rest quietly amongst the shadows.

STARGAZING

It feels like magic, looking up, watching stars switch on, one by one, like pinpricks in a blanket. Thousands of new stars are being born every second, and thousands are dying too. Some of the stars we see are memories – of light burning, time travelling. It may seem impossible to tell them apart, at first, but pick out a pattern or a brighter star and the mysteries of the universe will start to unfold.

Stars are so far away it takes years for their light to reach us. Some of the stars we see may have already died. Winter is a great time to stargaze because it becomes dark early. You don't need a telescope, just a warm blanket.

If you can see a bright star, you may be looking at a planet. Jupiter has a yellow hue; Mars is tinged red and Venus is white. Other bright stars include Polaris (the North star) and Sirius (the Dog star).

You could be lucky and see a meteor shower. A meteor is a space rock that enters the Earth's atmosphere and breaks up, creating a shower of burning light – a shooting star!

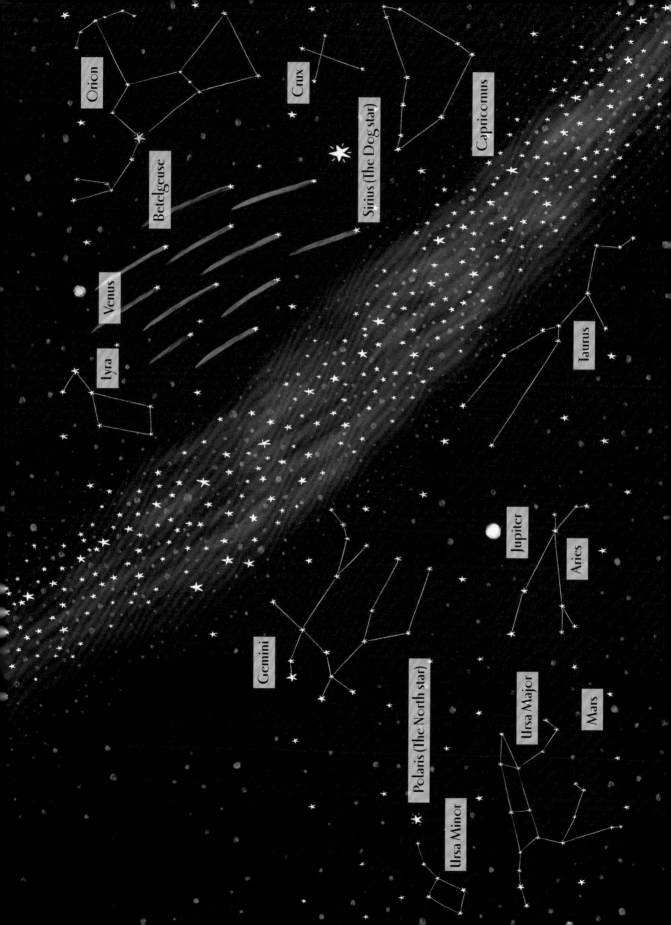

A LONG SLEEP

· ·

The brown bears hug inside their den, chipmunks curl up underground, snakes snooze in a tangle of tails, bats huddle upside down, hedgehog sleeps in a bed of leaves. They'll stay there until the wild, whistling wind gives way to a warm spring breeze.

A hedgehog builds a winter shelter made out of dead leaves, twigs and feathers. The twigs are tightly woven together to keep the heat in during the long, cold months.

Bats huddle together in dark, damp caves and other winter roosts. During hibernation, a bat's body temperature will lower so they need to roost in cool places. Caves are a great place to hibernate as they stay at a constant temperature.

Brown bears build up a thick layer of fat by eating and eating before hibernation, so they can survive through the winter months, waking when the weather warms up.

Sometimes travelling great distances to an established den, garter snakes overwinter together in large groups. Coiling themselves together helps them to maintain body heat.

Chipmunks collect and bury acorns to feed on in the winter. They curl into a small ball in an underground tunnel and eat from their collection of nuts while they wait for winter to end.

· ·

GARDENS
OF THE
WORLD

GARDENS AROUND THE WORLD

Humans have known for thousands of years how to shape nature. We can take a seed and choose where to plant it. We can trim and sculpt a plant so it grows the way we want it to look. We mow lawns, create designs with flowers; we even shape bushes to look like giant animals. Wherever you find humans, you'll find the gardens we create. Each garden tells you a lot about the person who designed it: some prefer big, dramatic gardens, others prefer winding walkways and cosy nooks to sit in; some like to control every leaf and petal, others prefer to keep things wild.

We can have fun with gardening, and we can also use our skills to help plants. When we trim a tree (the gardener's word is "prune"), we remove badly placed or weaker branches so the tree will grow better. We can try to stop a plant from being eaten by animals. And many gardeners garden in ways that help the environment, thinking of clever ways to save water or feed pollinating insects, for example.

Over the following pages, you can explore some very different gardens from around the world. Some of the gardens you may like and others you may not. Gardening is a personal choice and, just like art or fashion, we all have our own taste. But spending time in gardens is calming, and it's often the spark we need to start our own green-fingered adventures.

GARDENS BY THE BAY, SINGAPORE

Singapore's futuristic Gardens by the Bay is like a nature fantasy land. It has metal Supertrees that light up, a 4D ride that lets you experience the flight of a dragonfly, and the Flower Dome – the largest glass greenhouse in the world.

Singapore is known as the Garden City. In 1967, the late Prime Minister Lee Kuan Yew filled public spaces with new trees and lush greenery to create a calm space for people who lived in and visited the city.

Fast forward forty years and a new prime minister decided that wasn't enough. Lee Hsien Loong announced Gardens by the Bay would transform Singapore from a "Garden City" to a "City in a Garden". The 250 acre nature park is bigger than 180 football pitches.

There are many high-tech attractions in the gardens but there are tranquil spaces, too. This green space might inspire you to add some solar lights and drama to your own planting adventures.

PETERHOF, RUSSIA

Peterhof Palace is surrounded by manicured gardens, artificial lakes and grand fountains that send water cascading in to the sky. Peter the Great built Peterhof Palace in 1709 to rival Louis XIV of France's Palace of Versailles. He wanted to show Europe that Russia was a rich and powerful superpower too.

The gardens have marble walkways and shining bronze-gilded statues. The biggest statue is a giant, hulking Samson prying open a giant lion's mouth – a symbol of Russia's victory in war.

Peterhof also shows how nature can be tamed into precise shapes. Viewed from the sky, the gardens are amazingly symmetrical. Peterhof could inspire you to add water features or symmetry to your garden – even if you're starting with a window box or terrarium design.

JARDIN MAJORELLE, MOROCCO

Jardin Majorelle is an oasis in the desert city of Marrakech. You can escape the midday sun by walking beneath banana trees, through bamboo groves and next to marble fountains.

The painter Jacques Majorelle created the garden in 1924. It's full of artistic flair with dramatic plants and brightly-coloured paints that cover buildings, walkways and plant pots. It shows how a garden can really reflect someone's personality.

The most famous part of the garden is Majorelle's studio, a villa he painted electric blue. The shade is even named after him – blue Majorelle. The villa is surrounded by cacti with the same towering plants repeated over and over again.

The garden was later owned by famous French fashion designer Yves Saint Laurent. He and his partner bought the garden in the 1980s to restore and look after for future generations to enjoy. Will you be inspired by Jardin Majorelle? You could paint pots with vibrant colours and start your own cacti collection.

RHS GARDEN WISLEY, UK

The Royal Horticultural Society (RHS) garden at Wisley has always been home to gardening experiments. It combines garden designs of the past and future in one lush space in the English countryside.

The original garden was the creation of George Fergusson Wilson – a businessman, scientist, inventor and keen gardener. Wilson tried new ways of planting and tested growing exotic plants. You can visit his water garden designs, featuring irises, water lilies and other bog plants.

At Wisley, you can visit glasshouses with rainforest, desert and cloud forest plants, a one-hundred-year-old Alpine rock garden, an arboretum (collection of trees) as well as vegetable and fruit fields. Will Wisley inspire you to have a go at growing new plants?

Today, Wisley uses science to explore how plants and our gardens can adapt to extreme weather, pollution, pests and diseases.

NATURE AND YOU

WHAT IS A GARDEN?

· ·

When we think of having our own garden, we may picture an outdoor space with a striped lawn and beds of colourful flowers. But a garden is any area in which you can grow and enjoy your own plants. You can create a glorious garden on a balcony or on a window ledge. Even indoor rooms can be used to create green spaces, and these give you the exciting option to grow tropical and desert plants. You're only ever limited by your own imagination.

Gardening is good for you

The calming processes of tending to a new seedling, tasting a freshly popped pea or smelling a fragrant rose all help to keep you focused on the here and now. Being in touch with the day-to-day rhythms of nature reminds us of our place in a wider world. For all of these reasons, and more, studies show that getting elbow-deep in soil has a positive impact on a person's well-being. And, the interesting thing is, you don't have to garden outside. People who keep house plants are just as likely to feel calm and happy. In fact, even looking at a photograph or a view of nature can create positive feelings.

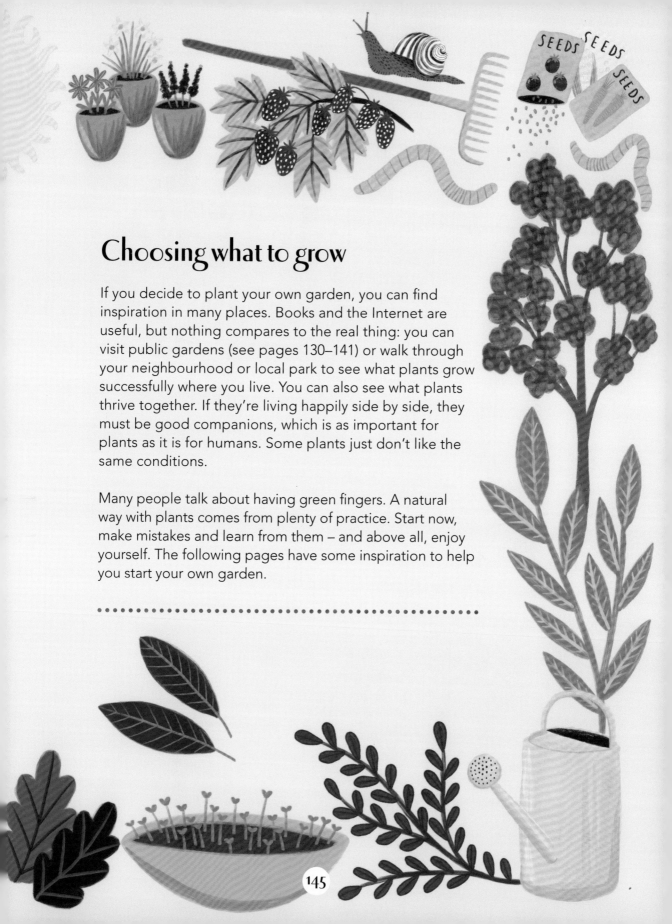

Choosing what to grow

If you decide to plant your own garden, you can find inspiration in many places. Books and the Internet are useful, but nothing compares to the real thing: you can visit public gardens (see pages 130–141) or walk through your neighbourhood or local park to see what plants grow successfully where you live. You can also see what plants thrive together. If they're living happily side by side, they must be good companions, which is as important for plants as it is for humans. Some plants just don't like the same conditions.

Many people talk about having green fingers. A natural way with plants comes from plenty of practice. Start now, make mistakes and learn from them – and above all, enjoy yourself. The following pages have some inspiration to help you start your own garden.

Enjoying green spaces

It doesn't matter if you live in the countryside or in a high-rise block of flats, there are plenty of ways to calm your senses with the magic effect of plants.

House plants

When you start growing plants indoors, you'll see your home in a whole new light. A sunny and steamy bathroom transforms into a rainforest when you fill it with moisture-loving plants. Some plants are good at removing pollutants from the air so having them in your home can improve your physical health as well as your mood.

Terrarium

You can create the conditions of a desert in a glass terrarium, so it's a good choice for succulents or cacti. And because you're choosing where to position the young plants, it's a fun way to express your creativity. Most cacti and succulents like bright sunshine and they don't like a lot of water. Buy cactus soil to keep your new plants happy.

TOP TIP: try to do some research before you choose your plant and match where the plant came from to the space you're putting it in. Think about how much light it will get and how humid it is. Persevere – there's a plant to suit every space.

Plant a window box

This compact plot is the perfect size to show off your personality with plants that appeal to the senses. You could choose to grow edible plants like lettuce or strawberries, fill the box with wildflowers to attract the hum of pollinating insects, or grow hyacinths if you like flowers with a scent.

TOP TIP: the important thing with a window box is to get the watering right. It's a good idea to wet the compost and then let it dry a little before you water it again.

Park

If growing your own plants isn't an option, stepping outside to enjoy a local green space has a positive effect on your mental well-being. Everywhere, even the biggest city, has a park to stroll through. Breathe deeply, feast your eyes, fill your nose with garden scents and listen to what's happening around you. See if you can identify which bird is singing, make a beeline for a wildflower meadow or visit a duck pond to stay in touch with the creatures who live in your area.

TOP TIP: buy coloured gravel to cover the surface of the soil and experiment with adding other creative touches, such as pebbles or small toys.

Grow flowers

If we all plant wildflowers, we'll create colourful highways for bees, butterflies and other pollinators to travel along instead of the improved farmland we've replaced wildflower meadows with. It's no sacrifice to dedicate a space to these blooms. Flowers make a rainbow of your garden as the flowers themselves are brightly coloured and, of course, so are the creatures who love to visit them. If you don't have an outdoor space, you could try growing them in a window box instead.

Create a bird feeder

You may put out a bird feeder with the feeling you'll only be helping birds. But just wait – as soon as a feathered family starts visiting your feeder, you'll be hooked. People who feed birds are a little bit selfish. Having birds nearby is so enjoyable!

TOP TIP: to make a bird feeder, take a clean, empty milk or soft drink bottle with the lid still on and ask an adult to help you make a hole in the side so birds can get to the seeds. Fill the container with bird seed to just below the opening and tie it from a tree or somewhere else to hang.

Travel by bike

Cars are noisy and pollute the air so they're best saved for longer journeys. Using pedals to power you from one place to another is a smarter choice. You're more likely to notice the passing of the seasons if you're out in nature every day, and nothing beats the freedom you feel when you climb on your bike and ride along with the wind on your face. It's good for your body and your mind as well as the planet.

Clean our beaches

The litter that makes its way to our rivers and beaches doesn't just spoil the view – it can be harmful to the wildlife who live there. It can pollute the water and some animals can get tangled up in plastic packaging. Lots of beaches run events for volunteers to help pick up litter. All you need is a pair of gloves and a bin bag to help out.

Protecting nature

Over the centuries, the changes made by humans has had a negative effect on nature. We've paved over meadows, chopped down trees, polluted rivers and confused wildlife with noisy and bright cities. We can each play our part in protecting nature. Plus, it's lots of fun.

REDUCE
REUSE
RECYCLE

Reduce, reuse, recycle!

You can protect the planet by stopping your rubbish from going to a landfill. Try not to use throwaway cups, spoons and straws; recycle whenever you can – and try to think of creative ways to use anything that would be thrown away. Did you know you can turn a yoghurt pot in to a plant pot for seedlings? Just make holes in the bottom to let water drain out.

You've reached the end of your book, but this is just the beginning of your journey. Seek each habitat, flower and creature in these pages, explore a park or woodland, river or sea. And create your own garden, so the magic of nature touches you each and every day.

GLOSSARY

adaptation
A skill or physical change that has helped a species survive their changing environment. See **evolution**.

asteroid
Made of a combination of rock and metals, that orbits around the Sun. See **orbit**.

bacteria
Tiny organisms that live on, in and around most living and non-living things. Some can be harmful and cause disease.

bloom
To produce a flower.

bulb
A rounded underground part of some plants which allow them to store leaves and buds safely during harsh conditions, such as winter.

chlorophyll
Chemical found in plants, it enables a plant to absorb and convert the energy of sunlight, carbon dioxide and water into sugars.

compost
A type of soil, good for growing plants in. Garden compost for adding to soil is made from a mixture of rotting matter, such as leaves, kitchen scraps and grass. Potting compost is good for growing plants in containers.

continent
A large mass of land – Earth has seven continents.

crustacean
A type of animal that has a hard outer body, most are aquatic, such as lobsters, crabs and shrimps, but some crustaceans, such as woodlice, live on land.

deciduous
Plants and trees that lose their leaves at certain times of the year, such as oak trees and maple trees.

evaporation
The process through which liquid turns into a gas or vapour.

evergreen
Plants and trees that keep their leaves all year round, such as holly.

evolution
The gradual change of species over time as they adapt to their environment.

flower
The part of a plant that blooms, has petals and makes fruits or seeds.

fossil
The remains of a plant or animal that has been preserved in rock.

germinate
When a seed begins to sprout.

gravity
A naturally-occuring force which attracts one object to another and prevents things from floating away in to space.

habitat
The natural home of a plant or animal.

hibernation
A type of extended sleep that some animals go in to during winter, to save energy.

larvae
The juvenile form of some insects and some animals.

migration
Movement of animals from one area of the world to another. Many species migrate to leave harsh conditions, such as winter, drought or food shortage.

nocturnal
Animals that are most active at night.

orbit
The path an object, such as a planet, takes as it circles around another.

parasite
An organism that lives on or inside another creature. Some parasites can cause disease.

pollen
Fine grains produced by the male parts of flowers that combine with the female parts of plants to produce seeds.

pollination
The process where pollen is moved from a male part to a female part of a plant, or between plants, so the plant can produce seeds.

pollinator
Animals that cause pollination to happen by transferring pollen, such as bees, bats and birds. Some plants are pollinated by the wind.

pollution
The introduction of material that is harmful to the environment.

predator
An animal that hunts and eats other animals. See **prey**.

prey
A creature that is a source of food for other animals. See **predator**.

root
The part of the plant which gives it support by attaching it to the ground. The roots also carry water and nutrients from the soil to the rest of the plant.

solar system
The Sun together with its orbiting (see **orbit**) planets, such as Earth, and smaller objects, such as **asteroids**.

species
A group of living organisms consisting of similar individuals capable of producing offspring, for examples lions or Scots pine trees.

venom
A sometimes lethal substance produced and injected by animals, such as snakes, spiders and scorpions. Commonly used to subdue prey, some animals use venom as a defence mechanism to protect themselves.

· ·

INDEX